W9-BSV-604

Mrs. Kasprzyk

written by
M. C. Helldorfer

illustrated by
Alexi Natchev

ATHENEUM BOOKS FOR YOUNG READERS

Atheneum Books for Young Readers
An imprint of Simon & Schuster Children's Publishing Division
1230 Avenue of the Americas
New York, New York 10020

Text copyright © 1997 by Mary-Claire Helldorfer
Illustrations copyright © 1997 by Alexi Natchev

All rights reserved including the right of reproduction in whole or in part in any form.

Book design by Angela Carlino
The text of this book is set in Veljovic Medium.
The illustrations are rendered in pen-and-ink and watercolor.

Printed in the United States of America
First Edition
10 9 8 7 6 5 4 3 2 1

Library of Congress Cataloging-in-Publication Data
Helldorfer, Mary-Claire.
Harmonica night / by M. C. Helldorfer ; illustrated by Alexi Natchev.—1st ed.
p.   cm.
Summary: One by one, members of a family join in a nighttime frolic on the beach.
ISBN 0-689-80532-2
[1. Seashore—Fiction. 2. Family members—Fiction.]
I. Natchev, Alexi, ill. II. Title.
PZ7.H37481Har   1997
[E]—dc20
93-40669

8. VI. 1996

For Aunt Margie—who loves the sea

—M. C. H.

For Varvara—the ocean of my youth

—A. N.

Lights out. Moon on.
I lie in bed and hear the
sea. *Rush-hush. Rush-
hush.* Is nobody awake?
Nobody—but the moon
and the sea and me.

And Gramma—her hair bright as tinsel!
She smiles at me, then puts her finger to
her lips. We tiptoe down the wooden steps.

The beach feels soft. I run to meet
the rushing sea. The moon has tossed
a silver net. With her toe, Gram pulls
its shimmering edge.

Shells have slipped through the moon's bright net, and smooth, wet stones.

"Treasure, Gram!"

She finds a starfish and lays it on my arm.

Bending close to the sea, we cannot hear a door open. . . .

Ambush! Who let out
the dog?
    Harlow goes moon-
dipping, then shakes and
turns and shakes. He's
salty dry; Gram and I,
gritty wet.
    Who let you out, boy?

Uncle Pat.

In his pajamas and hat, he weaves across the sand. "Ahoy, mates!"

"Yo ho ho," I answer, and climb on an overturned guard chair. Tonight we sail the pirate seas.

Uncle Pat lifts his hands, curling them into a spyglass. He turns toward the house. "Ghost coming with the breeze, mates. Hope she be bringing good luck."

My sister, Nina, her pale gown blowing, brings aboard kisses.

And bad luck, too!

"Aground, aground!" Uncle Pat shouts. He climbs overboard and backstrokes across the sand.

"Where are we? Send out a search party. Question that fisherman!"

Aunt Jane casts a long silver line to hook a fish, or the moon.

"Welcome to Sea Monster Isle," she says, then whispers in my ear, "Don't look behind you."

"Mom?"

"Monster!" She winks at me, then shakes her seaweed head and waves her seaweed arms. "I'm carrying you off to my undersea cave," Mom says, covering me with slithery stuff.

"Help—somebody—help!"

Harlow howls at the sea creature. Uncle Pat searches for a monster net. Gram and Nina cast moon spells, but the monster won't let go of me.

Suddenly a big white towel leaps between us—*whippity whip!* I'm free.

Grandad dries off Mom and me. He says, "I've heard that campfires keep sea monsters away. And juice, and peanut butter crackers." We sit close around the flames, munching and watching the moon get fuzzy.

"Feels like a harmonica night," says Aunt Jane.
Uncle Pat pulls the silver bar from his pocket. The
sea is suddenly quiet, the big moon gone.
"Duet with a foghorn," Uncle Pat announces,
playing one more song before we go inside.

Gram tucks me in. Harlow jumps onto the bed, smelling like a whole ocean.

I can hardly hear it now, *rush-hush,* hardly hear it . . . *rush.* Hear it, Gram?

Shh.